Myst

MW01228704

Theresa Marrama

Copyright © 2022 Theresa Marrama

Cover art by digitalhandart

Interior art by digitalhandart

All rights reserved.

No part of this publication may be reproduced, stored in a retrieval system, or transmitted, in any form or by any means (electronic, mechanical, photocopying, recording or otherwise), without prior written permission from Theresa Marrama.

ISBN: 979-8-9857821-5-8

"Art enables us to find ourselves and lose ourselves at the same time."
— **Thomas Merton**

TABLE OF CONTENTS

ACKNOWLEDGMENTS

A big **THANK YOU** to Molly Bogart for her wonderful translation of this story and to Dave Bailey for taking the time to edit this story!

Prologue

Everything is black. Everything is silent. Stephen is silent. There aren't any people in the museum. Stephen is completely alone. He's a little scared. He's also a little anxious… He thinks about all the stories of his best friend, Paul. Stephen thinks about his teacher… and when his teacher will discover that he's not with the group! Oh my!

Stephen slowly walks in silence when suddenly he sees a painting. Immediately, he understands. It's THE painting. It's the Mona Lisa! He looks at it in silence. Everything is black but he can see…its eyes. He slowly walks towards the painting. When he walks towards the Mona Lisa, he doesn't look at its eyes. He looks at the ground. Finally, he arrives in front of the most famous painting in the world.

At that moment, Stephen hears a noise. He panics! He thinks about the mummy! He thinks about his conversation with Paul when he said, *"Did you know that the museum is haunted? Yes, there's a mummy that haunts the museum! The mummy that haunts the museum is named Belphegor. There is also a woman who haunts the museum. A lot of people think that the Mona Lisa also haunts the museum at night."*

Its eyes! It seems like she is looking at him! The Mona Lisa looks at Stephen intensely.

Was it a bad idea? He thought that his idea was good, but not at this moment!

Chapter 1

Stephen Wants to go to the Louvre

Stephen lives in France. He lives in Paris, the capital of France. In France, there are a lot of museums. The museums in Paris are very famous. There's the Orsay Museum, the Orangerie Museum, the National Museum of Modern Art, the Louvre Museum, and many others.

Everybody goes to the museums to look at the art. Museums are interesting and important to Stephen. Going to a museum is necessary to understand the culture of France. There are a lot of paintings, sculptures, and other forms of art in museums.

Stephen wants to go to a specific museum. He wants to go to the Louvre to see the most famous painting in the world. He wants to see the Mona Lisa. He also wants to see the most famous statue in the world. He wants to see the Winged Victory.

Stephen's mother told him that the Mona Lisa was a small painting. Stephen's father told him that the painting was not an ordinary painting. Stephen wants to see the painting. He wants to see it with his own eyes. His teacher told him that it's not an ordinary painting, it's a painting that is interesting and bizarre at the same time.

Stephen has a friend. Paul is his best friend. Paul goes to museums often. Paul thinks that the museums in France are stupid, but his parents force him to go to them. Paul doesn't think that art is interesting. But Stephen doesn't think art or museums are stupid. He thinks that museums are interesting and that art is important.

Stephen looks at art a lot at school, in books, and on the Internet. Stephen likes to look at art on the Internet. Stephen likes all forms of art. But he wants to see the art of the Louvre. He wants to have his own experience at the Louvre Museum and see the most important art in France.

Stephen heard a lot of interesting stories about the Louvre. Stephen really wants to go to the Louvre. Paul often goes to the Louvre. Paul sees a lot of art at the museum. Stephen never goes to the Louvre or other museums in Paris because his parents work a lot.

Stephen wants to see the art with his own eyes. He wants to go to the Louvre Museum.

Chapter 2

His Friend Paul

At 5:30 P.M., Stephen arrives at his friend Paul's house. Paul lives in a small apartment near the school. Stephen thinks that museums are fascinating. He thinks that a trip to the museum is fascinating. He wants to discuss the museum with his friend Paul.

"Hi, Paul," says Stephen.

"Hi," responds Paul.

Paul and Stephen go into the living room. Stephen is impatient. He wants to talk about the Louvre. He wants to ask a lot of questions and listen to all the stories Paul has about his visits to the Louvre Museum.

"Paul, you've visited the Louvre, right?"

"Yes, I visit it often," responds Paul.

"Do you go to the Louvre often? I want you to explain to me all the things you saw at the Louvre, please!"

Paul doesn't want to discuss the museum or the art. He doesn't want to discuss his experiences at the Louvre. Paul's parents like to go to the Louvre, but not Paul. Paul is not interested in museums or art, but he knows that Stephen is very interested in the Louvre. He begins to explain his experiences. Stephen listens well and thinks that everything Paul says is interesting. Paul doesn't think it's interesting.

"Oh Stephen, I have a lot of stories about the Louvre. I go to the Louvre all the time. I go there all the time with my parents. The other day, I was in the Louvre Museum, and I saw the Mona Lisa and all sorts of sculptures. Did you know that the museum is haunted?"

"Huh? The Louvre is haunted?" asks Stephen.

"Yes, there's a mummy who haunts the museum! The mummy who haunts the museum is called Belphegor," explains Paul.

Stephen listens to Paul attentively.

"Huh? There's a mummy that haunts the museum?" asks Stephen.

"One day, I saw a form walk in front of me. I looked attentively and I'm sure that I saw something bizarre. I'm sure that I saw the MUMMY! I was surprised, very surprised. But maybe it was just my imagination." "You saw the mummy?" asks Stephen. "Were you afraid?"

"No, I was not afraid, but I was surprised," responds Paul.

Stephen really wants to go to the Louvre. Paul recounts another one of his experiences in the Louvre Museum and Stephen listens attentively.

"The Louvre is fascinating. But some say that you can only see the ghosts that haunt the museum at night."

"You saw the mummy at night?" asked Stephen interestedly.

"Yes, it was at night!"

Stephen doesn't know much about the museum. He listens to Paul, and he is very surprised and very interested. After the conversation with Paul, he's really interested in the Louvre!

Stephen says to him, "Paul, I really want to go to the Louvre."

"You've never been to the Louvre?" asks Paul.

"No, I've never been to the Louvre and I've never seen the Mona Lisa!" responds Stephen.

"Really?" asks Paul, surprised.

"Yes, really. My parents work a lot, but I want to go there!" responds Stephen. "My parents have told me a few of the things that are in the Louvre Museum. Do you like art? Do you think that museums are interesting?"

"No, for me, art and museums are not interesting. But I think that the mummy that haunts the Louvre is interesting! The mystery of the Louvre is interesting! There's also a woman, the most important woman of the Louvre Museum: the Mona Lisa! A lot of people think that the Mona Lisa haunts the museum at night," responds Paul.

Stephen is fascinated by everything Paul is telling him. He reflects for a moment in silence, and he says, "I want to go to the

Louvre and I want to see the Mona Lisa and all the art with my own eyes!"

"I think that the class is going to the Louvre. The art teacher goes to the Louvre Museum each year with his class," explains Paul.

"Really?" asks Stephen, interestedly.

"Yes, I am sure of it," says Paul.

Chapter 3

Belphegor the Mummy and the Mona Lisa

After his visit to Paul's house, Stephen returns to his house. He thinks about his conversation with Paul. He thinks that his stories about the Louvre are very interesting! He thinks of the Mona Lisa and of the mummy, Belphegor. He is fascinated by the story of the museum and by the ghosts that might haunt the museum.

He goes to look for his laptop. On his laptop, he begins to look for some information on the museum, on Belphegor the mummy and on the Mona Lisa.

Stephen looks at a lot of photos of the museum. Stephen looks at some photos of some of the large rooms in the museum and he is fascinated. He looks at the paintings and the sculptures. He looks at a lot of different art. Stephen knows that the museum has a lot of art. He looks for the most popular form of art at the Louvre and he discovers that the Mona Lisa is the most viewed painting in the world. He thinks of his conversation with Paul, *"A lot of people think that the Mona Lisa haunts the museum at night."*

Did Paul really see a ghost at the Louvre? Is it possible to see the ghost of a mummy if one visits the museum at night? If Paul thinks he saw a ghost at the museum that night, one can surely see a ghost at the museum at night!

He continues to read some articles on the museum. He discovers an interesting article about the mummy, Belphegor. He begins to read the article,

According to a lot of people who work in the Louvre Museum and a lot of tourists as well, there is a mysterious form who walks in the rooms and corridors of the Louvre. This mysterious form haunts the rooms of the museum. A lot of people think that this form is Belphegor the mummy. No one has seen this form during the day. This form is only visible at night. It's a mystery, a big mystery.

Stephen can't believe his eyes! He cries, "One can only see this form at night!"

He continues to search for more information on the Mona Lisa. He reads an article that says,

There are, in fact, three Louvre Museums in the world. There is the Louvre that is found in Paris, a Louvre Museum in

Lens, in the North of France, and another in Abu Dhabi.

Stephen is fascinated by the article. "There are three Louvre Museums! This is interesting!" Stephen thinks. He continues to read,

The Mona Lisa is a fascinating painting. This painting is also a little mysterious. When one looks at the painting, it seems that she looks at you as well. Her eyes seem to penetrate you. Her eyes continue to look at you even if you don't look at her. One doesn't know if she haunts the museum or if her stare haunts the people who look at her. It's a mystery. It's the mystery of the Louvre.

Stephen doesn't stop thinking about Paul and his story about the Louvre at night. He wants to explore the Louvre at night. He wants to look the Mona Lisa in the face! He wants to see her stare! Maybe he can even see a phantom!

Chapter 4

Stephen Has an Idea

The next day Stephen wakes up. He wakes up with an idea. He thinks that he has a good idea. Stephen has a different idea. It's not a good idea. He doesn't want to just look at the art at the Louvre. He has another idea! He wants to explore the Louvre at night and search for a ghost.

Stephen goes to school. He's in class when his teacher announces, "This weekend, the class is going to go to the Louvre! We are going to visit the most famous museum in the world!"

Finally! He can see the Mona Lisa face to face, with his own eyes.

Stephen can't concentrate the rest of the day. He is completely obsessed with his idea to explore the Louvre at night and with the announcement in class: A VISIT TO THE LOUVRE!

He can't comprehend why Paul doesn't like museums. He wants to persuade Paul to explore the museum with him at night. He wants to explain to him that he found a lot of information about the museum and that one can see ghosts in the Louvre at night.

After school, Stephen goes to the house, and he enters the living room to talk with his dad. His dad asks him, "What are you doing, Stephen?"

Stephens responds, "Dad, have you ever visited the Louvre? I talked with Paul. Paul goes to the museum all the time with his parents. He told me that the mummy Belphegor and the Mona Lisa haunt the museum!"

His dad looked at him with a serious expression. He says to him, "Yes, I have been there. The Louvre is not haunted, and ghosts do not exist. Stephen, you have a big imagination."

"The Louvre is interesting! Dad, there are more than fifteen thousand people who visit the Louvre each day! It's interesting, no?" says Stephen with enthusiasm.

His dad looks at Stephen and responds, "Yes, Stephen, it's very interesting."

"Dad, did you know that the Louvre is the most visited museum in the world? It's incredible, no?" says Stephen.

"Yes, Stephen. It's a museum with a lot of important art," explains his dad.

"Dad, I found some articles online about the Louvre and there are some people who think that they also saw a ghost."

"A ghost. It's absurd, Stephen!" says his dad.

Stephen doesn't respond because he is distracted. He thinks about the ghosts and of his dad's response, "Stephen, the Louvre is not haunted, and ghosts don't exist. You have a big imagination." Why does his dad not think that the museum is haunted? Is it because he does not have a big imagination?

After his conversation with his dad, Stephen wants to talk to Paul. He goes to his bedroom. He wants to explain his idea to him. He grabs his cellphone to write a text to Paul,

> *Paul, I have a good idea! I want to explain it to you!*

Stephen wants to go to the museum with his class but there is a problem: his teacher is not going to like his idea. His teacher is not going to be happy if he explores the museum at night without the group!

Chapter 5

What an idea!

The next day, Stephen wakes up and immediately looks at his cellphone. He sees a text from Paul. The text says,

What idea? Tell me!

Stephen thinks about his idea. He wants to explain his idea to Paul, but he can't explain it over text.

He quickly goes to the living room and sees his dad. He asks him, "Dad! Dad! Can I go to Paul's house after school today?"

"No, Stephen, you have to do your homework after school."

"Dad, please!"

His dad doesn't respond immediately. He looks at Stephen seriously.

"Dad, I can do my homework at Paul's house after school? Please…"

His dad thinks and finally says to him, "OK, but you must show me your homework tonight when you return to the house. Do you understand?"

"Yes, I understand."

A moment later, he runs to his bedroom. He grabs his cellphone and writes a text to Paul,

After school, I can explain my idea to you at your house!

After a moment, there is a text from Paul,

> **OK, after school!**

Suddenly, his dad enters his bedroom. He says to him, "Stephen, you must go to school! Let's go!"

"Yes, dad! I'm coming," responds Stephen.

Chapter 6

His Idea

Stephen goes to class, but he can't concentrate. He's obsessed with his idea about the Louvre.

After school, Stephen goes to Paul's house. Immediately, when he enters Paul's house he hears, "Stephen, what's your idea?"

"I have a good idea!" responds Stephen.

"Tell me!" exclaims Paul.

"This weekend when we go to the Louvre, I want to separate from the group to explore the museum at night! Do you want to explore the museum with me?"

"Huh? You want to stay at the Louvre alone at night?" asks Paul.

"Yes! It's a good idea, right?" asks Stephen.

Paul doesn't respond. He looks at Stephen, when suddenly he hears, "Paul? You must do your homework! Come to the kitchen with Stephen!" says Paul's mom.

The two boys go to the table in the kitchen to do their homework. Stephen can't continue his conversation with Paul because his mom is in the kitchen. Stephen is not interested in his homework. He thinks about his idea. It's an excellent idea! He thinks about the Louvre. After some time, Stephen looks at the time. It's 6:00 P.M. Stephen puts his homework in his bookbag and whispers, "Paul, what do you think about my idea?"

"I think that your idea is impossible. Ha, ha, ha…" whispers Paul.

"Huh? Why is my idea impossible?" asks Stephen.

"I have already visited the Louvre at night. It's impossible to explore the museum alone. There are guards and security everywhere in the museum."

"It's possible! I am going to think of a plan!" responds Stephen.

—

Stephen returns to his house. He is determined to come up with a plan. He looks on the internet and searches for photos and maps of the museum. While he looks at them, he has a lot of ideas. He thinks of a plan, and he imagines how he is going to separate from the group at the Louvre at night.

While he surfs the internet, he sees a lot of maps of the museum and a lot of information about the museum. He sees an article that says,

No one can be in the museum alone at night. It is forbidden!

Stephen asks himself, "Why is it forbidden to be in the museum at night? Maybe no one can be in the museum at night because of the mummy and the ghosts?"

At that moment, he sees a map of the museum that doesn't resemble the other maps of the Louvre. The map of the museum says, "In order to see the mummy Belphegor". He can't believe his eyes. He says to himself, "There's a map of the museum in order to see Belphegor the mummy?!"

He begins to look at the map of the museum when he hears his dad yell to him, "Stephen, it's 9:00 P.M.! Go to bed!"

Stephen puts his laptop on the ground. He looks at his phone. He is fascinated with that article and with the photo of the map of the museum online. He writes a text to Paul,

I saw an interesting map of the museum on the internet. I can explain it to you tomorrow!

Chapter 7

The Laptop

The next day, Stephen wakes up and immediately grabs his laptop. He looks at the map of the Louvre. Stephen understands that the map of the museum is not a normal map. The map of the museum is different. He needs a copy of the map. But how? He has an idea! He can print a copy of the museum map at school. It's not a good idea to print the museum map at his house. His dad might see it.

He puts his homework and his books in his book bag. He hears his phone. He grabs it and he sees a text from Paul.

What museum map?

Stephen yells loudly, "What Museum map? The most important museum map in the world!"

At that moment, he goes to the door to leave his bedroom when all of a sudden, his dad responds, "The most important museum map in the world? What are you talking about, Stephen?"

Stephen panics! He thinks quickly and says, "The map of the museum... the most important map for the class...of history!"

"Stephen, do you have your laptop?"

Stephen doesn't respond immediately. He looks at his laptop on the bed. He can see the map of the museum... Oh no, the map of the museum! He doesn't want his dad to see the map!

At that moment, his dad enters his room.

"What are you doing, Stephen?" asks his father.

"Huh? Nothing…"

"Stephen, do you have your laptop?" His dad looks at the bed and sees the laptop.

"Yes," responds Stephen, panicked.

He doesn't want his dad to see the map of the ghosts at the Louvre.

"What are you looking at on the internet?" his dad curiously asks him.

"Oh… just some information about the Louvre… for a field trip," responds Stephen nervously.

His dad grabs the laptop and says to him, "You have to go to school, and I have to go to work! Let's go!"

"Yes, dad! I'm coming," Stephen responds nervously.

His dad leaves Stephen's bedroom. Stephen quickly grabs his phone and leaves his bedroom.

Stephen quickly gets in his dad's car. In the car, Stephen is silent. He doesn't talk because he's thinking about the map of the museum. He wants to explore the Louvre. He is a little bit anxious... and if his teacher discovers his plan...?

Finally, he arrives at school. His dad says to him, "Goodbye, Stephen. Don't forget to call me after school!"

"Yes, goodbye."

At that moment, Stephen grabs his phone and sees a text from Paul.

> *Are you at school? I am in front of the cafeteria.*

Stephen puts his phone in his bookbag and quickly enters the school.

Chapter 8

The Map of the Museum

Stephen is anxious! He thinks about the map of the museum on his laptop, and he says to himself, "That's a problem! My dad is going to see the map!"

"Stephen, what do you want to explain to me?" asks Paul impatiently.

"I think that I have an idea in order to explore the museum at night!" whispers Stephen.

"Huh? How? Tell me!"

"Yes, I can explain everything, but I must go to the library to print the museum map that I found online. Do you want to go with me?" asks Stephen.

"The museum map? I don't understand," responds Paul.

"Let's go. I'm going to explain everything."

The two boys go to the library. In the library, Stephen explains everything to Paul. He explains everything about the map.

"Stephen, why do you want to print a map of the museum? What museum map?" asks Paul impatiently.

"Paul, I have an idea in order to explore the museum at night!" whispers Stephen.

"Huh? How?" asks Paul.

"Yes, I found a map of the Louvre on the internet. But not just a map of the museum, a map to see a ghost at the museum! It's incredible."

"I don't understand," responds Paul.

"Don't worry! I have a good idea!" responds Stephen.

Stephen finishes printing the museum map at the library. He puts the map in his book bag and the two boys go to class.

After school, the two boys attentively look at the map of the museum. They talk about the map and about the museum. They talk about their idea to separate from the group.

Finally, Stephen and Paul return to their houses. At home, Stephen goes to his bedroom to do his homework. He looks at the map of the museum a lot, and finally, he puts the museum map in his book bag and goes to bed.

—

The next day, at 5:00 P.M., his dad announces that they are going to go to school for the field trip. Stephen, happier than ever, grabs his book bag without seeing the map of the museum fall to the ground. He runs to his dad's car.

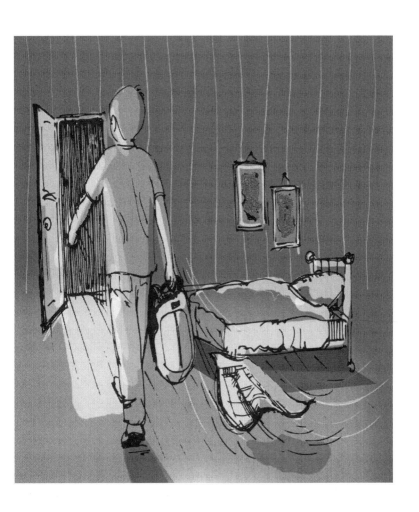

chapter 9

A Problem

A few minutes later, Stephen arrives at school. It's time to go to the Louvre.

In the car, his dad says to him, "Stephen, do you have everything for the field trip?"

"Yes, dad!"

"O.K. Have fun!"

"Thank you, dad."

Stephen sees Paul in front of the bus and walks toward him.

"Hi, Stephen! Do you have the map of the museum?" says Paul.

"Hi, Paul! Yes, I have the map!"

At that moment, Stephen searches for the map in his book bag. He starts to panic a little. Paul sees that he's a little panicked.

"Stephen, why do you seem anxious?" asks Paul.

"Paul! The museum map isn't in my book bag! I'm sure that it was there."

"You don't have the map!" cries Paul. "Where is the map?"

"I don't know. OH NO, I can't explore the museum without the map!" exclaims Stephen.

At that moment, the two boys hear their art teacher say, "O.K., let's go! On the bus!"

Paul looks at Stephen, panicked, and there's a moment of silence. The two boys climb on the bus and at that moment, Paul says, "I have an idea!"

Paul grabs his phone and looks at it in silence for a moment.

"You don't have the map of the museum, but don't panic, I have another idea," explains Paul.

"What other idea?" asks Stephen.

"I am going to find the map of the museum online on my phone," explains Paul.

"Oh, what a good idea, Paul!" exclaims Stephen.

After a few minutes, with the help of Stephen, Paul finds the same map of the museum on his phone. He saves the photo of the map on his phone. On the bus, the two boys talk about the museum map and about the plan to explore the museum at night.

"Paul, in a few hours, it's possible that I'll see a ghost. I can't wait!" explains Stephen.

Finally, at 6:00 P.M., the bus arrives in front of the Louvre.

Chapter 10

At the Entrance of the Louvre

On the bus, the art teacher announces, "O.K. everyone, listen! In a moment, we are going to enter the Louvre Museum. It's important that each person gives me their phone. It's forbidden to have phones in the museum! Everyone must listen to the guide during the tour."

Stephen and Paul look at each other. Stephen looks at Paul's phone. It seems like Paul is a little panicked. Stephen panics as well and whispers to Paul, "Did you hear that? You can't have your phone in the museum!"

"Yes, I heard," responds Paul.

"What are we going to do? It's impossible to explore the museum at night and to see a ghost without a map of the museum!" says Stephen.

At that moment, Paul looks at his friend with a serious expression and says, "Stephen, it's not impossible if I have my phone. Give me your book bag."

Stephen doesn't have time to think. He gives his book bag to Paul.

Paul quickly puts his phone in it.

"O.K. everyone, let's go!" says their teacher.

The two boys walk toward the entrance of the museum when the teacher asks them, "Phones, please."

"I don't have my phone with me," Paul responds immediately.

"And you, Stephen?"

Stephen doesn't say anything. He's anxious, but he gives his phone to the teacher in silence.

Stephen walks, and at that moment he sees... the PYRAMID! It's the glass pyramid! The glass pyramid of the Louvre! It's incredible! Stephen can't believe his eyes. For him, it's incredible that a lot of people didn't like this pyramid when it was constructed. He saw on the internet that the pyramid was constructed in 1986 by a Chinese American architect named I.M. Pei.

He looks at the pyramid. At that moment, he's not thinking about ghosts! He looks at the museum attentively.

"The museum is incredible!" exclaims Stephen.

"Stephen! Listen to me!" says Paul.

"Huh? Oh, yes, I'm listening to you," responds Stephen.

"We have to verify the idea for us to separate from the group," says Paul.

"Paul, we can verify the idea: we are going to wait. When the group leaves the museum, we are going to hide in the bathroom," explains Stephen.

The art teacher announces to the students, "O.K. everybody, if you have a bag or a book bag, enter with me. The security guards are going to search the bags. The others enter with Mrs. Dupont."

Stephen and Paul look at each other. Paul looks at Stephen's book bag. He notices that Stephen is a little panicked.

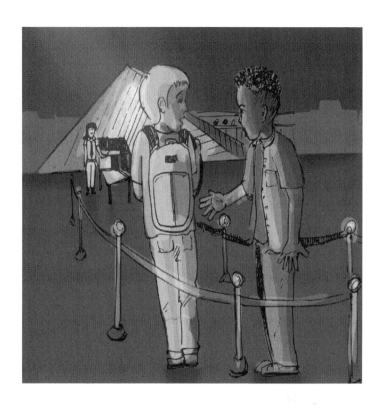

"Did you hear that? The security guards are going to search our bags!" says Stephen.

"Yes, I heard that," responds Paul.

"Paul, your phone!" says Stephen, panicked.

Chapter 11

In the Louvre Museum

Stephen walks with the others who have a book bag and he's anxious. He continues to look at Paul behind him. It's his turn to give his book bag to the security guard. The security guard looks at Stephen and says, "Put your book bag on the table, please."

Stephen slowly puts his book bag on the table. At that moment, he sees his teacher who's looking at him attentively. He panics and his hands tremble. The security guard opens his book bag. Stephen looks at his teacher with wide eyes. The guard looks inside when suddenly, another security guard yells to her, "Alain, come see, please!"

Stephen can't believe his eyes! The guard didn't see the phone! He can accomplish his plan! A few minutes later, he enters the Louvre with Paul and the group.

"Paul, the guard didn't see your phone in my book bag! It's incredible!" says Stephen.

"I know, now we have the map of the museum and a good idea," responds Paul.

The group walks for two hours from room to room to look at paintings, sculptures, and a lot of other types of art. The group listens to the art teacher explain the history and the importance of the art.

Stephen now knows why the Louvre Museum is in an ancient royal palace. The palace is enormous, and the Louvre has an enormous collection of art! At that moment, the group looks at the Winged Victory. Stephen looks at the sculpture and he is fascinated.

After that, their teacher announces, "Now, everyone, we are going to enter the room of the Mona Lisa! It's the last room of our visit. The most famous painting in the world! Normally, there are a lot of tourists in this room! It's important to stay together."

Stephen and Paul look at each other. The two wait a minute and when the group enters the room, they run to the bathroom.

"Attention, please! Everyone must leave the Louvre in 10 minutes. Thank you for your visit and good night!"

Stephen looks at Paul in silence. He is a little anxious. Paul says to him, "Stephen, look at the phone, what time is it?"

Stephen opens his book bag and looks at Paul's phone for the time. But there's a problem— the phone isn't working.

"Paul, there's a problem with your phone! The battery isn't charged!" explains Stephen, panicked.

Paul looks at him but doesn't respond.

"Paul, did you hear that? The phone isn't working!" says Stephen.

"Yes, I heard that," responds Paul.

"Paul, what are we going to do?" asks Stephen, panicked.

"I don't know! We can't explore without a map, but we don't have a choice!" exclaims Paul, panicked.

They wait patiently in silence in the bathroom for a long time.

Suddenly, everything is black.

"Do you think everyone has left?" asks Stephen.

"Yes, everything is dark and I don't hear anyone."

The two boys leave the bathroom when suddenly, they hear a noise. Stephen looks at Paul with wide eyes. His hands tremble. Stephen looks at Paul and he seems anxious too.

Chapter 12

Mystery at the Louvre

"I'm going to check that we are alone in the museum!" says Paul, panicked.

Stephen looks at him with a serious expression and says, "O.K., but quickly."

Paul walks into the corridor. Stephen waits for Paul. Finally, he sees a silhouette in the distance.

"Paul, is that you?"

But nobody responds. The silhouette doesn't walk. At that moment, Stephen thinks, "Is it possible? Is it Belphegor the mummy? No, it's just Paul!"

He runs toward the figure and yells, "Paul! It's me, Stephen."

The silhouette isn't there anymore. Stephen doesn't understand. The silhouette has disappeared.

Everything is black. Everything is silent. Stephen is silent. There aren't any people in the museum. Stephen is completely alone. Where is Paul? He is a little scared. He is also a little anxious. He thinks about all of Paul's stories. He thinks about all the information that he found on the Internet. He thinks about his teacher... When his teacher is going to discover that he isn't with the group! Oh my!

He walks slowly in silence and suddenly he sees a painting. Immediately, he understands. It's THE painting. It's the Mona Lisa!

He looks at it in silence. Everything is black but he can see... it's eyes. He walks slowly toward the Mona Lisa. When he walks toward the painting, he doesn't look at its eyes. He looks at the ground. Finally, he arrives in front of the most famous painting in the world.

At that moment, he hears a noise. Stephen panics! He thinks about the mummy! He thinks about his conversation with Paul who said, "Did you know that the museum is really haunted? Yes, there's a mummy that haunts the museum! The mummy that haunts the museum is named Belphegor. There's also a woman who haunts the museum. A lot of people think that the Mona Lisa haunts the museum at night as well."

It's eyes! It seems like she's looking at him! The Mona Lisa looks at Stephen intensely. Stephen is paralyzed by her stare.

Was this a bad idea? He thought that his idea was good, but not now!

He hears another noise behind him. He turns around slowly. In front of him, he sees a silhouette. He looks at the silhouette.

He starts to run in the other direction when he hears, "What are you doing in the museum at night? It's forbidden! Come here now! Your friend is already with me. What were you thinking? You can't explore the museum at night! It's forbidden!"

Stephen stops immediately. He is paralyzed with fear. This isn't the mummy! It's a security guard! At that moment, he understands that it was a bad idea, a very bad idea to explore the museum at night.

ABOUT THE AUTHOR

Theresa Marrama is a French teacher in Northern New York. She has been teaching French to middle and high school students since 2007. She is the author of many language learner novels and has also translated a variety of Spanish comprehensible readers into French. She enjoys teaching with Comprehensible Input and writing comprehensible stories for language learners.

Theresa Marrama's books include:

Une Obsession dangereuse, which can be purchased at
www.fluencymatters.com

Her French books on Amazon include:

Une disparition mystérieuse
L'île au trésor:
Première partie: La malédiction de l'île Oak
L'île au trésor:
Deuxième partie: La découverte d'un secret
La lettre
Léo et Anton
La Maison du 13 rue Verdon
Mystère au Louvre
Perdue dans les catacombes
Les chaussettes de Tito
L'accident
Kobe - Naissance d'une légende
Kobe - Naissance d'une légende (au passé)
Le Château de Chambord : Première partie : Secrets
d'une famille
Zeinixx
La leçon de chocolat
Un secret de famille
Rhumus à Paris
Rhumus se cache à Paris

Her Spanish books on Amazon include:

La ofrenda de Sofía
Una desaparición misteriosa
Luis y Antonio
La Carta
La casa en la calle Verdón
La isla del tesoro:Primera parte: La maldición de la isla
Oak

La isla del tesoro: Segunda parte: El descubrimiento de
un secreto
Misterio en el museo
Los calcetines de Naby
El accidente
Kobe - El nacimiento de una leyenda (en tiempo
presente)
Kobe - El nacimiento de una leyenda (en tiempo pasado)
La lección del chocolate
Un secreto de familia
Rhumus en Madrid

Her German books on Amazon include:

Leona und Anna
Geräusche im Wald
Der Brief
Nachts im Museum
Die Stutzen von Tito
Der Unfall
Kobe - Geburt einer Legende
Kobe - Geburt einer Legende (Past Tense)
Das Haus Nummer 13
Schokolade
Avas Tagebuch
Rhumus in Berlin
Verschollen in den Katakomben

Her Italian books on Amazon include:

Luigi e Antonio
I calzini di Naby
Rhumus a Roma

Check out Theresa's website for more resources and materials to accompany her books:

www.compellinglanguagecorner.com

Check out her digital E-books:

www.digilangua.co

Made in the USA
Columbia, SC
19 June 2024

37014244R00041